# The Adventu...

# ARNIE the DOUGHNUT

## BOWLING ALLEY BANDIT

written and illustrated by

# LAURIE KELLER

Christy Ottaviano Books

Henry Holt and Company 🦴 New York

# CHAPTER 1

What's that?

I think it's a sprinkle!

#11

#10

Hey, Mr. Bing, do you remember the time you tried to EAT me?

#9

I sure do, Arnie!

It seems like just yesterday that Mr. Bing brought me home from the Downtown Bakery and tried to eat me. Time sure flies. And look at us now—Mr. Bing and his trusty DOUGHNUT-DOG!

**YUP**, since Mr. Bing decided not to make me his **BREAKFAST** (Phew!), he decided we should think of something **ELSE** he could make of me. Coming up with ideas was easy, but agreeing on one was **ANOTHER** story! I mean, would **YOU** want to be an **AIR FRESHENER** for someone's car?

Or a PICTURE FRAME?

And WHO in their right mind would want
to be a PINCUSHION?!

I guess I was hoping for something a *little* more glamorous.

Like being his **BALLROOM DANCE PARTNER.**

Or his **CHAUFFEUR.**

Or an **ENTERTAINER** at his parties.

Turns out he didn't like MY ideas any better than I liked HIS. We had given up trying and I was on my way out of town when Mr. Bing ran up to me with the doughnut-dog idea . . .

AND I LOVED IT!

But as popular as dogs are, we've discovered that some places don't like having dogs around—not even doughnut dogs.

We've worked our way around it, though. Sometimes I'm a doughnut-dog.

And sometimes I'm just a *doughnut*.

A chocolate-covered sprinkle doughnut, that is!

But there's one thing that never changes— Mr. Bing and I are ALWAYS best friends.

# CHAPTER 2

Mr. Bing LOVES to bowl. He and three of his friends are on a bowling-league team called the BINGBATS. Tuesday is their league night, and Mr. Bing always lets me go with him to watch. I didn't think I'd like going to the bowling alley, but now Tuesday is my favorite night of the week!

MONDAY NIGHT — WOMEN'S LEAGUE
TUESDAY NIGHT — MEN'S LEAGUE
WEDNESDAY NIGHT — MIXED LEAGUE
THURSDAY NIGHT — ROBOT LEAGUE

Come down now, Arnie!

# I like hanging out with the Bingbats.

Kenny

Bernie

Howard

Mr. Bing/Walter
(Team Captain)

# Maybe it's because they all remind me of . . .

Drum roll, please!

# DOUGHNUTS!

Take BERNIE for instance. He's the classic GLAZED DOUGHNUT. He's popular and mellow and wears shiny "glaze" in his hair. And when he bowls, he slides on his shoe like it's coated with sugar!

Then there's HOWARD. He's the good ol' JELLY DOUGHNUT. He's sweet and jolly and when he rolls a strike, it makes the alley shake like a bowl full of jelly!

KENNY is the LONG JOHN of the group.

Pardon me, but I much prefer LONG JONATHAN, just as I'm sure Kenny prefers KENNETH.

He's tall and thin, and his bowling moves are as smooth as the creamy filling in a Long John!

And finally, MR. BING—he's the CINNAMON TWIST. He looks plain at first, but his personality has a surprising "spice" to it. And when he releases the ball, his arm does a little TWIST over his head!

I've made lots of **OTHER** friends at the bowling alley too. In fact, between the bowling balls, bowling pins, and rental shoes I've made

8 HOMIES,

11 PEEPS, and

13 BFF's!

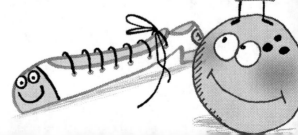

They've taught me pretty much everything I need to know about the game of bowling.

 # LiKE:

* When a bowler knocks down all the pins in ONE try, it's a **STRIKE**.

* When a bowler knocks down all the pins in TWO tries, it's a **SPARE**.

* When a bowler doesn't knock down ANY pins, it's called a **GUTTER BALL**.

## Oh, and the most important one:

* When a bowler takes off his smelly bowling shoes, **RUN FOR YOUR LIFE!**

IT'S TRUE! WE STINK!

P-U!

But of all the great things about the bowling alley, my favorite is that there's a restaurant inside called the BOWL-O'-CHOW and they have a KARAOKE MACHINE! I usually watch Mr. Bing bowl for a while, and then I wander over to the BOWL-O'-CHOW to sing a few songs. I was scared to try it at first, but now I'm a regular!

Here he is—the little doughnut who put the *O* in *KARAOKE*. Let's give it up for Arnie the Doughnut!

Woo Hoo!

Thanks, everybody!

Yay, Arnie!

Here are a few of my old standbys:

And I always end with my signature song:

# CHAPTER 3

I'm not saying that I've never run into trouble at the bowling alley.

Hey, Peezo!

I've told you before—no doughnuts allowed at the bowling alley!

Well, what are ya gonna DO about it?

I'll SHOW ya what I'm gonna do about it!

OW!

Quit it!

In case you're wondering if **I'M** a bowler . . . I'm **NOT**. Doughnuts don't usually make very good bowlers. It's a **SIZE** thing.

Help! I'm a chocolate-covered sprinkle pancake!

The average doughnut weighs only **1.8 ounces,** and the smallest bowling ball weighs only **6 pounds.**

+ = **IMPOSSIBLE**

But Mr. Bing is the **PERFECT** size for bowling. And he's gotten so good at it that this year he decided to buy his very **OWN** bowling ball.

Oh, that was ANOTHER one of Mr. Bing's ideas for me—to be his new BOWLING BALL!

In the past, Mr. Bing always used one of the bowling-alley balls that anyone can use. His favorite was a 13-pounder named **BRUISER** from the wrong side of the racks (where the extra-rough-and-tough bowling balls live).

What's it TO ya, ERNIE?

He always calls me ERNIE!

But his new, purple bowling ball, BETSY, weighs a WHOPPING 15 POUNDS!

# HOLEY DOUGHNUT!

I just broke RULE #17 in the *Bowling Alley Rules and Regulations Handbook*:

## RULE #17:
## UNDER NO CIRCUMSTANCES SHALL ANYONE (not even cute little doughnuts) MENTION THE WEIGHT OF A FEMALE BOWLING BALL.

And that's exactly what I did. I blurted it out as casually as if I were saying that Mr. Bing owns a pair of pink, poodle boxing shorts!

Thanks for sharing that, Arnie!

Excusez-moi for interrupting, but Monsieur Arnie has made a big FAUX PAS (pronounced "FO-PAH"). It is the French word for, how you say, HE IS IN DEEP DOO-DOO.

(Le French Cruller)

Just wait till Betsy finds out. She'll have me banned from every bowling alley in the country!

# SHOWDOWN of the CENTURY!

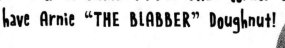

ladies and Gentlemen...in THIS corner we have Arnie "THE BLABBER" Doughnut!

And in THIS corner we have Betsy the "Let Him Have It" purple bowling ball!

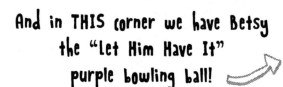

It looks like Arnie is making the first move.

AMAZING! He actually APOLOGIZED to Betsy! Well, here's where she'll really let him have it!

# UNBELIEVABLE!

She just told Arnie that she's **PROUD** of her 15 glorious pounds and she doesn't care **WHO** he tells!

# They're actually LAUGHING about it!

Well, just when I thought I'd seen it all. Its looking like a WIN-WIN for this showdown tonight, folks!

# CHAPTER 4

So tonight is a VERY

**BIG**

night for the Bingbats. They're competing in the 62nd Annual Lemon Lanes Bowling Championship! There are eight teams in the men's league, and for the past six years the Bingbats have finished in second place. And for the past six years the team that beat them is **The Yada-Yada.**

Steamer
(Team Captain)

Bubba

Rupert

Frank

But **THIS** year the Bingbats have the most points so far. If they can hang on to their lead until the end of the night, that **FIRST-PLACE TROPHY** will be theirs!

Since it's such an important night, I have a **BIG** surprise planned, and it involves one of my FAVORITE things to do—

# SINGING!

I got the idea from going to a baseball game with Mr. Bing. (It was the same day I caught a fly ball. It stuck right to my frosting!)

During the seventh inning, the crowd stands to do the Seventh-Inning Stretch and sings "Take Me Out to the Ball Game" together:

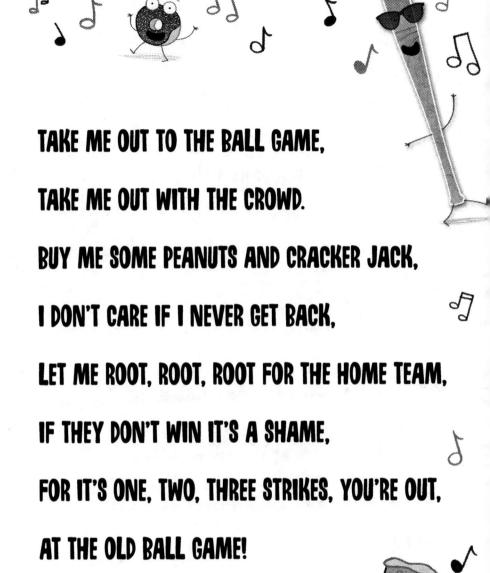

TAKE ME OUT TO THE BALL GAME,

TAKE ME OUT WITH THE CROWD.

BUY ME SOME PEANUTS AND CRACKER JACK,

I DON'T CARE IF I NEVER GET BACK,

LET ME ROOT, ROOT, ROOT FOR THE HOME TEAM,

IF THEY DON'T WIN IT'S A SHAME,

FOR IT'S ONE, TWO, THREE STRIKES, YOU'RE OUT,

AT THE OLD BALL GAME!

# FUN, RIGHT?

So, here's my plan. There are three games in the tournament, and I thought that during the SEVENTH frame of the SECOND game we could all do the Seventh-FRAME Stretch!

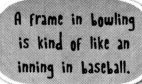

A frame in bowling is kind of like an inning in baseball.

But instead of singing

## "TAKE ME OUT TO THE BALL GAME,"

we'll sing

## "TAKE ME OUT FOR SOME BOWLING!"

I love it!

When I told Ms. Marlene, the manager at the BOWL-O'-CHOW about the Seventh-Frame Stretch, she suggested moving the karaoke machine out to the bowling alley so everyone could read the words on the big screen! I loved her idea, but I worried that the karaoke crowd would be upset not being able to use it that night.

**WHAT?!**

**NO KARAOKE TONIGHT?!**

**I've been practicing in the shower ALL WEEK!!!**

Look, Grandma, that man is NAKED! And SOGGY!

Ms. Marlene said it wouldn't be a problem, because on championship night everyone likes to watch the bowlers, so the restaurant is practically empty anyway. The only "bowling folks" who DIDN'T seem excited about the Seventh Frame Stretch were the yada-yadas. In fact, they acted kind of **GROUCHY** when I told them.

Hey, Ernie, maybe the Yada-Yadas are grouchy because the Bingbats are in the lead and they're NOT.

Could Bruiser be RIGHT? Are the Yada-Yadas really grouchy because the Bingbats are in the lead and they're not? NOOOOOO, that's RIDICULOUS!

I know!

I bet they were grouchy because their SHOES were too tight! They sure LOOKED tight.

I tell ya, there aren't many things worse than shoes that are too tight. That's exactly why I don't wear them.

OH, THOSE POOR, GROUCHY YADA-YADAS AND THEIR ACHY FEET!

# CHAPTER 5

We just arrived at the bowling alley, and this place is **HOPPING!**

It reminds me of the morning I was made at the Downtown Bakery. The baker hung the **OPEN** sign in the window, and

The place was swarming with customers!

The tournament has officially begun! It's so exciting! But I have something to confess. While the Bingbats were busy putting on their bowling shoes, I dropped a few sprinkles in the thumbholes of their bowling balls. Not just ANY sprinkles, though. PINK sprinkles. Those are the LUCKY ones! I checked the rules and it's perfectly legal. So I figured a little good luck couldn't hurt on such a big night!

Between you and me, I'm glad he's using the PINK sprinkles. The BLUE ones make me so GASSY.

Now, I know it's early to be talking about trophies, but I want to show you my impersonation of the FIRST-PLACE TROPHY GUY.

PRETTY GOOD, RIGHT?

I don't see HOW he keeps his arms up like that all the time! If he comes home to live with us, I'm sure Mr. Bing would let him relax and put them down.

I'll bet Mr. Bing would even ask him to join us for dinner once in a while. BUT HE'D HAVE TO HELP WITH THE DISHES!

Please excuse me for just a minute. I need to run over to the bowling-ball return. I like being there every few frames to welcome the bowling balls back. The bowling-ball return sure looks like fun to ride on, but I hear it takes first-timers a while to get used to.

I don't think it would bother me, though. I figure if I can make it through the Ringy-Dingy Doughnut-Making Thingy© without getting sick, I can handle just about anything!

All the teams are bowling really well, but the Bingbats are still in the lead! The pins must be loving all the strikes the bowlers have been getting—they're flying all over the place! So far I've seen them do

head spins, CORKscrews, and AiR CHAiRS!

I know that because the pins taught me some of the breakdancing moves they do once a bowling ball smashes into them. I've gotten pretty good, but I really need to be more careful. Last time I did it, they told me I **BUSTED A MOVE.**

Sorry, guys!

# CHAPTER 6

The Bingbats won the first game! The second game is under way, and Mr. Bing just got his **THIRD STRIKE IN A ROW!**

I'll handle this.

Ya see, Ump, in *baseball* strikes are **BAD**, but in *bowling* they're **GOOD!**

They **ARE?**

In that case, sorry for the interruption. **GAME ON!**

Actually, three strikes in a row in bowling is called a **TURKEY!**

You don't say!

Well, it's almost time for the Seventh-Frame Stretch, so I'd better head over to the karaoke machine to warm up my pipes.

In honor of tonight's tournament, Arnie the Doughnut will now lead us all in

# †HE SEVENTH-FRAME STRETCH!

So, please stand, stretch, and sing along to

# "TAKE ME OUT FOR SOME BOWLING!"

That's my Arnie!

# CHAPTER 7

Well, I havent gotten the **OFFICIAL** word yet, but I'm getting the feeling that the Seventh-Frame Stretch was a **HIT!**

Encore!

Yay, Arnie!

I feel so refreshed!

Peezo, any thoughts on running for president?
Peezo, Are you dating Anyone?
Do you ever dance at chess games?
What a talent!
Tell us about your toppings, Peezo!
Peezo, Hollywood Calling!
HOLLYWOOD!
BRILLIANT!
That was just what I needed!
Peezo, Channel 9 News—I'd like to ask you a few questions...

# CHAPTER 8

Until this very moment, I thought finding out that doughnuts were made to be eaten was the only thing that could make my eyeballs do this:

It turns out that Mr. Bing throwing a GUTTER BALL makes them do that too!

# POOR MR. BING!

In all the time I've known him, he's NEVER thrown a GUTTER BALL. What could have HAPPENED? Oh, I have to be quiet—he's about to finish the frame. I'm sure he'll get right back on track.

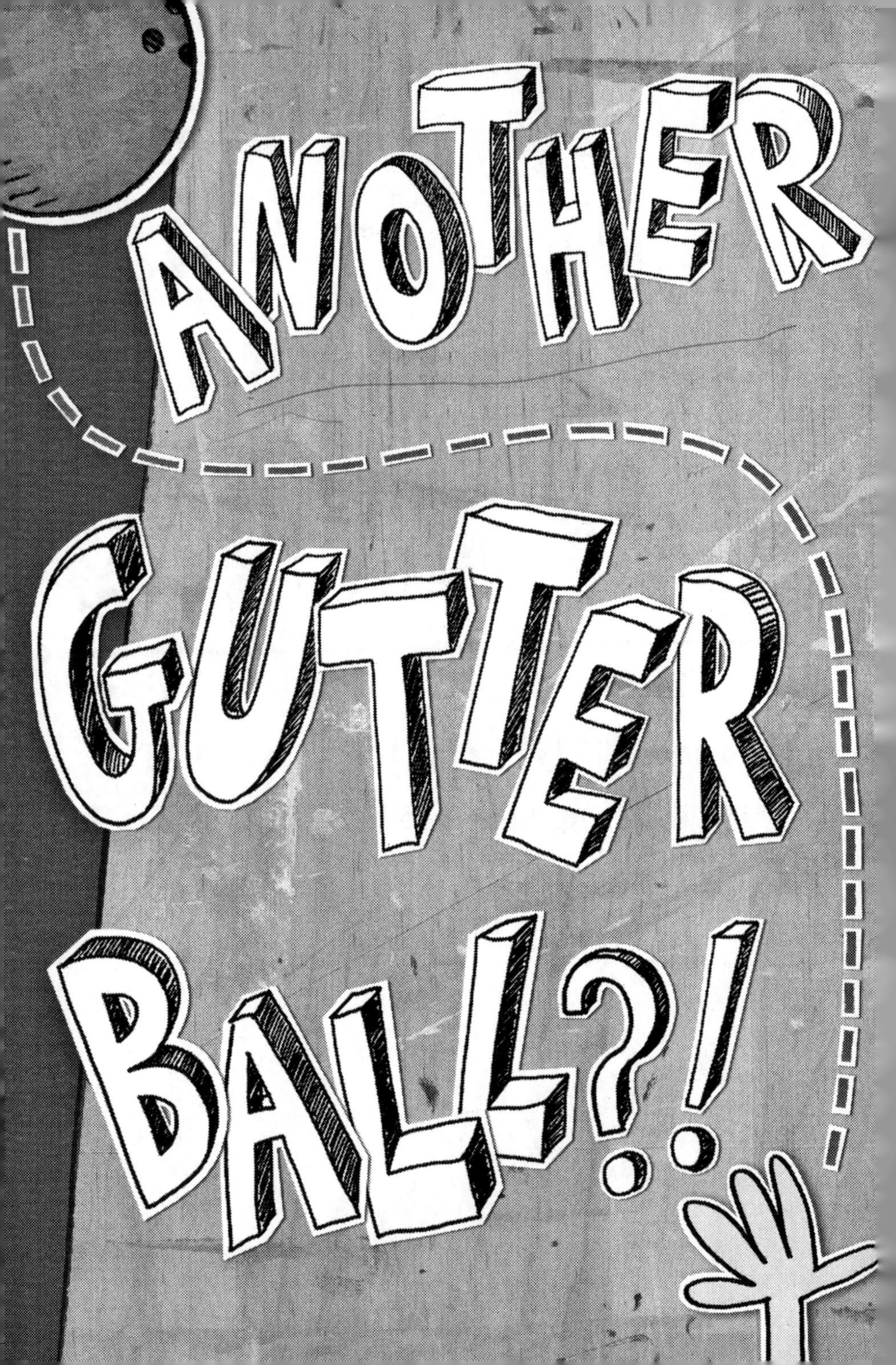
ANOTHER
GUTTER
BALL?!

# WHAT IS GOING ON?

## Mr. Bing did everything **EXACTLY** the way he always does:

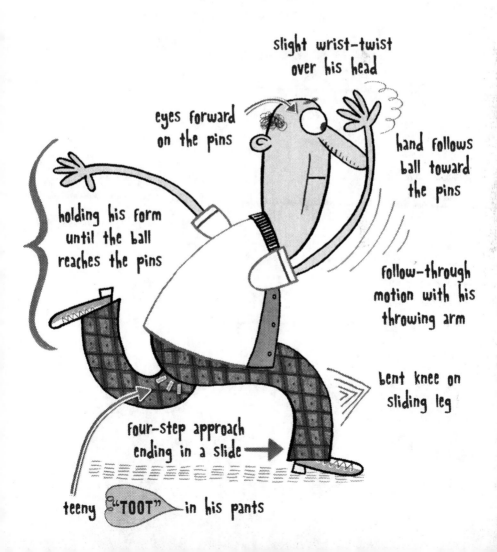

I'd better see if Betsy's all right after going into the gutter for the first time!

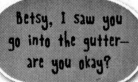

Betsy, I saw you go into the gutter— are you okay?

I'm FINE. I mean, it's not like I've never been in the gutter before, right, Ernie?

That's ODD. Betsy said she's been in the gutter before—but she HASN'T. And she called me ERNIE, just like Bruiser does.

OH, NO! BETSY'S LUCKY PINK SPRINKLES!

THEY'RE GONE!
TIPS
DUN DUN DUN
I didn't know the bowling alley had an organ player.
Me neither.

Betsy, what happened to your lucky pink sprinkles?

lucky pink sprinkles?

Yes, the ones I gave you before the tournament. Remember?

Oh, RIGHT—lucky pink sprinkles! uhhh... well, what HAPPENED was, errr... Someone STOLE them! Yup, someone stole them, all right.

WHO STOLE THEM?!

uhhhhhh...

that guy stole them— the grouchy one there!

# CHAPTER 9

# Steamer, the captain of the Yada-Yadas, stole Betsy's lucky pink sprinkles?

So, Bruiser was <u>RIGHT</u>—the Yada-Yadas ARE upset because the Bingbats are in the lead! Well, that explains their grouchiness and dirty looks and why they didn't want to take part in the Seventh-Frame Stretch—THAT'S WHEN THEY STOLE THE LUCKY PINK SPRINKLES!

Now that the Yada-Yadas have the lucky pink sprinkles **THEY'LL** have the extra good luck instead of the Bingbats. I have to get those sprinkles back without the Yada-Yadas knowing but HOW?

I know, Arnie! We can make disguises from stuff in the Lost and Found so the Yada-Yadas won't recognize us. Then we can sneak over to their lane and steal back the lucky pink sprinkles!

GREAT IDEA, PEEZO! I think that could work!

Look, Arnie—Steamer is on his way up to the counter right now! What should we do?
BE COOL—follow my lead!
LOST and FOUND
WHOOPIE PILLOW
GUM
To:

Well, I'm sorry for accusing you of stealing the lucky pink sprinkles. And I feel it's only fair for me to let you know we've been wearing disguises so you wouldn't recognize us. I'm really Mr. Bing's friend Arnie the Doughnut, and this is my friend Peezo.

WOW— you sure fooled me.

Well, WE'VE got some sprinkles to find and YOU'VE got to bandage up those disgusting feet and get back to bowling! Oh, and just so you know—in karaoke it doesn't matter HOW terrible you sing. EVERYONE is welcome!

# CHAPTER 10

# LEAPIN' LONG JOHNS!

Peezo and I were just walking past the bowling balls—the ones from the wrong side of the racks—and we overheard Rocky and Angus discussing something that stopped us in our tracks!

Hey, what's up with Bruiser painting himself purple?

I don't know, but he took off during that Seventh-Frame Stretch, mumbling something about getting back at that Bing guy and his new, purple bowling ball.

I wonder if this has anything to do with the phone call I got from Bruiser the other day. I didn't think much of it at first, but he sure had a lot of questions about the Seventh-Frame Stretch.

Hey, uh, Ernie . . . about your Seventh-Frame Stretch . . .
Oh, hi, Bruiser!
So, EVERYONE will be singing it together?
That's the plan!
How long will it last?
I'd say about two minutes, tops.
That's all, huh? Okay, thanks. OH, and tell Mr. Bing's new bowling ball GOOD LUCK for me. She's gonna need it, heh heh. I MEAN, since it's her first tournament and all.
Will do, Bruiser!
13

# WAIT A MINUTE...

Bruiser always calls me ERNIE. When Betsy called me Ernie, I thought it was because she was confused after going into the gutter for the first time, but that wasn't the reason AT ALL.

She called me ERNIE
because she's
not Betsy—

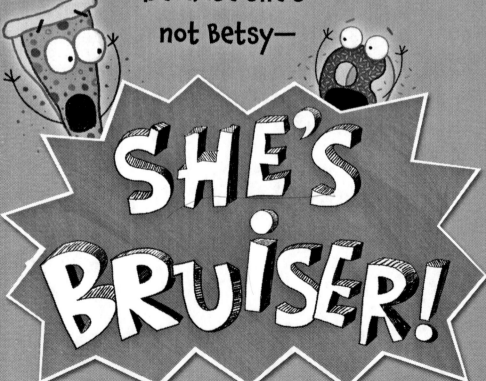

# SHE'S BRUISER!

All right, boys, you're on your own from here. I have to get back to the restaurant!

Ms. Marlene?

So Bruiser painted himself purple to look like Betsy—but where's Betsy?

Look, Peezo—Bruiser's wet paint left a trail. It runs all the way down the gutter of Lane 24 at the end of the alley!

# AHA!

That's why Bruiser asked about the Seventh-Frame Stretch. When everyone was singing, he rolled down the gutter and hid behind the lanes! Then he waited for Betsy to roll through, grabbed her, and took her place! And now he's rolling himself into the gutter every time Mr. Bing bowls! That means he's breaking Rule #61 in the *Bowling Alley Rules and Regulations Handbook*:

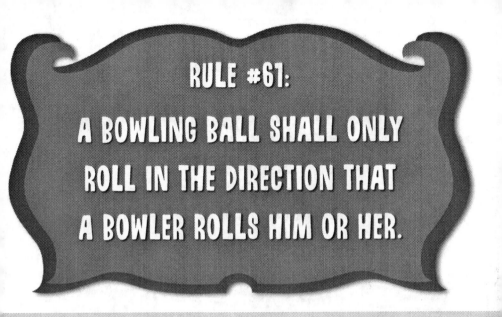

## RULE #61:

## A BOWLING BALL SHALL ONLY ROLL IN THE DIRECTION THAT A BOWLER ROLLS HIM OR HER.

I've got to get behind the lanes and follow Bruiser's paint trail so I can find Betsy and get her back into the game!

Okay, Peezo, on the count of three, give me a push!

ONE,

TWO,

THREE!

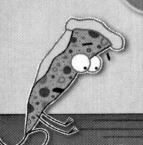

Bruiser's paint trail runs all the way behind Lane 10—the Bingbats' lane. This must be where he made the SWITCH!

LANE
10

HELP!
I'm being
BALL-KNAPPED!

His trail keeps going,
but it's getting thinner!

**OH, NO!** Bruiser's paint
trail **RAN OUT** and Betsy's
nowhere around! How will
I ever find her **NOW?**

And there's another one!

 And another one!

But where is the last sprinkle?

PING!

 OUCH!

**BETSY!**

She dropped her sprinkles so I could find her! BRILLIANT! But now I have to find a way to get her down. I wonder how Bruiser got her up there.

Hmmm mmmm mm mmm, mmm hmm mm hmm mm MMMM!

He used a ladder to get you up there but to make sure you didn't climb back down he gave it to a giant ladder-eating monster?

CHOMP! CHOMP! CHOMP! Mmmm, good ladder

We're going to have to jump! Don't worry, I'll catch you!

That's it—

a little more . . .

little more. . . .

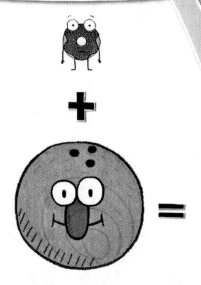

# CHAPTER 12

Peezo just called and said
that Mr. Bing is still throwing
gutter balls and that the
Bingbats are now three points
BEHIND the yada-yadas! There's
only one frame left, and the
only way the Bingbats can win
NOW is if Mr. Bing gets a
STRIKE. That way, he'll get
two BONUS ROLLS!

Come on, Betsy, we have
to catch Bruiser and get
you back in the game!

It looks like we got here just in time—

# HERE COMES BRUISER!

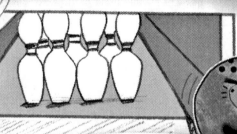

We twisted up my napkin like a rope so we can stop him!

Well, this is the moment of truth. Mr. Bing
has to get a strike to get the bonus rolls.
Now that Betsy's back with her lucky pink
sprinkles, at least he stands a chance. Here
he goes . . .

After all of Mr. Bing's gutter balls, he has to get a strike or a spare on the bonus rolls if the Bingbats are going to win the tournament.

## On BONUS ROLL 1—

HE GOT AN 8!

## And on BONUS ROLL 2—

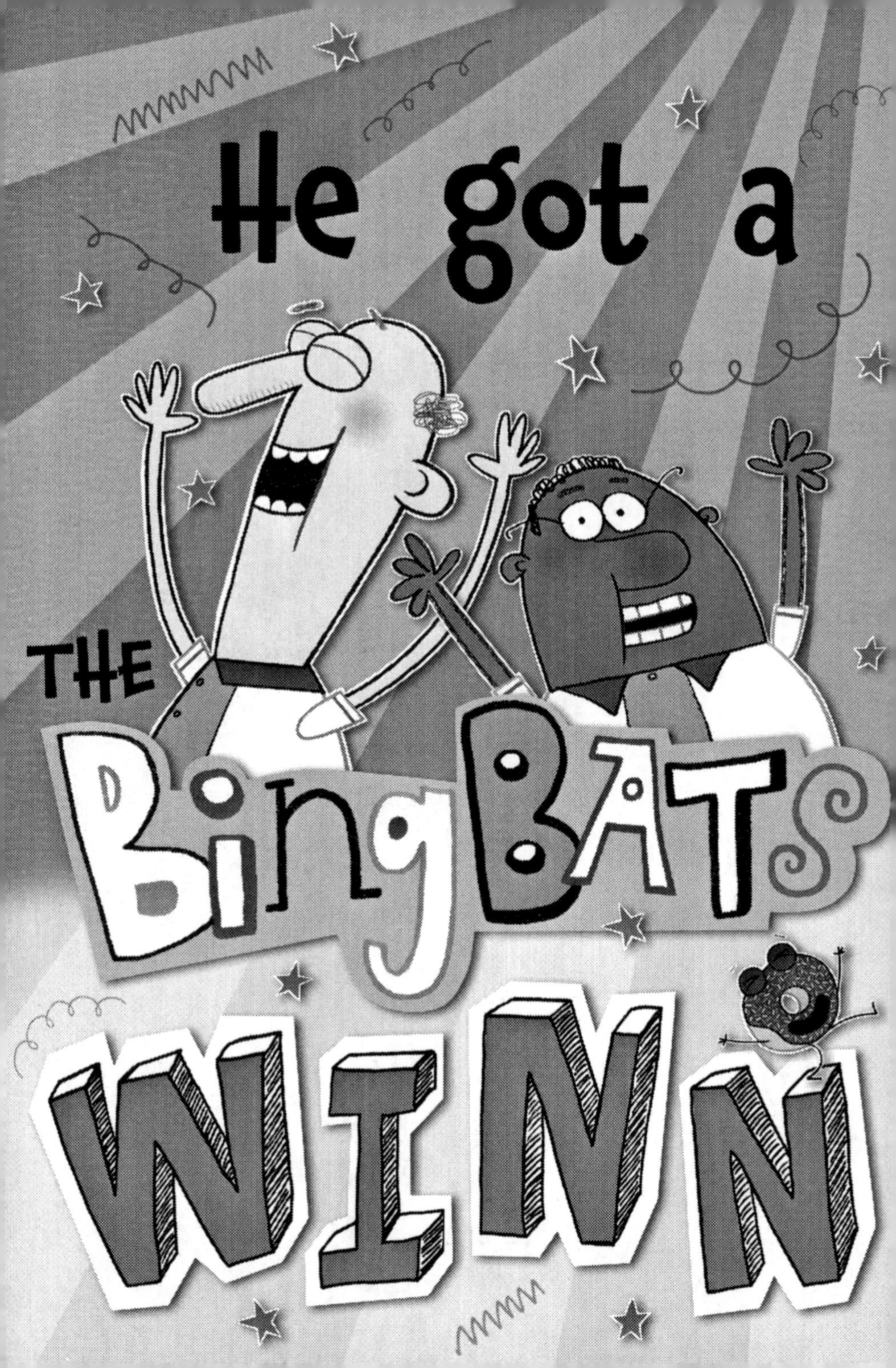
He got a
THE
BingBATS
WINN

The yada-yadas finished in second place. And no matter what Bruiser said, they don't seem upset about it at all.

Congratulations, Walter. Pardon my grouchy look—my shoes are killing me.

Thanks, Steamer.

That reminds me— **BRUISER.** I think we need to have a little talk.

# CHAPTER 13

So Bruiser—do you care to explain **WHY** you did what you did?

**WELL?**

I don't get it. You and Mr. Bing bowled together for years. How could you **DO** that to him?

How could I do that to **HIM?** How about what **HE** did to **ME**—dumping me for that fancy new bowling ball!

Excuse me, guys—I couldn't help overhearing.

Bruiser, you're a LEMON LANES BOWLING BALL! It's your job to help bowlers become so good that one day they'll buy their *OWN* bowling balls.

And that's what you did for Mr. Bing and lots of other bowlers. You're a GREAT bowling ball, Bruiser!

THAT'S THE MOST BEAUTIFUL THING I'VE EVER HEARD!

Come on, let's go to the party.

The party was off to a good start, but when Ms. Marlene said,

Hey, Arnie, KNOCK-KNOCK.

Who's there?

Kara.

Kara WHO?

KARAOKE-TIME, EVERYONE!

that's when things REALLY got rockin'!

Everyone in the bowling alley sang at least one song—even the Yada-Yadas! Boy, they weren't kidding about their singing voices.

But even more shocking than that, Bruiser apologized to Betsy, **AND** they sang several songs together!

As the evening wound down, Mr. Bing and I each had one special THANK-YOU to make before we left the bowling alley.

Mr. Bing found the perfect place to put Stiffy Stu McShiny. That's what I call him because he won't tell me his name! Stiffy Stu seems a little shy, but I think he'll loosen up a bit once he's lived with us for a while.

Let's take him with us on our walk tomorrow, Mr. Bing!

I figured as soon as we got him home he'd finally put his arms down, but he hasn't ONCE! He can't fool me, though. I bet he puts them down as soon as the lights go out. Watch this. . . .

I'll wait thirty seconds and flip the lights back on. . . .

I'll wait a whole
minute this time. . . .

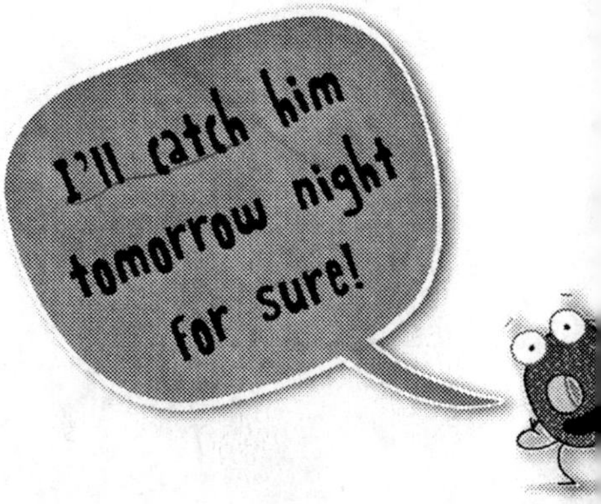
I'll catch him tomorrow night for sure!

[dedication tk]

Henry Holt and Company, LLC
Publishers since 1866
175 Fifth Avenue
New York, New York 10010
mackids.com

Henry Holt® is a registered trademark of Henry Holt and Company, LLC.

Library of Congress Cataloging-in-Publication Data
[TK]

ISBN 978-0-8050-9076-5

First Edition—2013
[ARTIST'S MEDIUM TK]

Printed in VENUE by PTR INFO
1  3  5  7  9  10  8  6  4  2